Wisdom

Jaya's Golden Necklace

a silk road tale   Peter Linenthal

Wisdom Publications, Inc.
199 Elm Street
Somerville, MA 02144 USA
wisdompubs.org

Library of Congress Cataloging-in-Publication Data
Linenthal, Peter, author.
  Jaya's golden necklace : a Silk Road tale / Peter Linenthal.
    pages cm
  ISBN 1-61429-232-9 (paper over board : alk. paper)
  1. Buddhism—Juvenile literature. 2. Buddhist stories. I. Title.
  BQ4032.L56 2015
  294.3—dc23
                    2015006368

ISBN 978-1-61429-232-6
ebook ISBN 978-1-61429-247-0

19 18 17 16 15
5 4 3 2 1

Cover and interior design by Gopa&Ted2. Set in Gill Sans 16/22.
Buddha and Hercules coins on page 38 are courtesy of the Pankaj Tandon
Collection. Buddhist text on page 39 is courtesy of the British Library.

Wisdom Publications' books are printed on acid-free paper and meet the
guidelines for permanence and durability of the Production Guidelines for Book
Longevity of the Council on Library Resources.

This book was produced with environmental mindfulness.

Printed in China.

For Phil, with much love,
and
for Gwen, inspired contributor.

P. L.

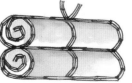

In the ancient city of Taxila, Jaya was upset with Mama.

"*No! Don't go!*" Jaya shouted, stamping her foot.

"But I must go, little one," said Mama.
"King Kanishka has ordered me
to bake my famous apricot cake
for his birthday party."

"While I'm gone, I want you to have something."

Mama unwrapped a small bundle.
Out fell a chain from which
dangled three gold coins.
Mama fastened the chain
around Jaya's neck
and kissed her cheek.

"My own mama gave
this golden necklace
to me, and now I
am giving it to you.
It will help you
when I'm not here."

Then, adjusting the tulip
in her own hair, Mama called
out as she left, "I promise,
I will see you soon!"

"Papa!" called Jaya, "Mama's gone to the palace to bake a cake for the King!"

Papa ran into the room. "I have orders from King Kanishka, too, little one. Listen."

Papa read from a fluttering scroll:

To Alexander, the best sculptor in Taxila:

I wish for you to carve a statue of the Buddha, the peaceful one, and bring it to my palace on my birthday.

Yours truly,
King Kanishka

"That gives me just two days!" gasped Papa.
"Will you help me pick out the best stone for the statue?"

"Of course, Papa."

They put on their sandals and ran to the stone yard.

The yard was full of gods and goddesses that Papa had carved,
but no one had ever carved a statue of the Buddha before.

"What does the peaceful one look like?" wondered Papa.

"I wish I knew!" said Jaya.

Varoosh!

Suddenly one of the coins on
Jaya's necklace started to sparkle
in the sunlight.

From out of the coin leapt Shiva,
lord of creation, dancing like
a silk scarf in the wind.

"You know what to do," Shiva said.

"Me?"

"You've watched your father carve all your life, little Jaya. Just start, and your ideas of peace will flow."

So Jaya started chiseling a huge stone.
Papa and Shiva joined her,
letting thoughts of peace
flow from their fingers
into the stone.

Chips of rock flew all night,
and the first rays of morning
light fell on a finished statue.

"It's beautiful!
Thank you, Shiva!"
exclaimed Jaya.

"The pleasure was mine!"

Then

Varoosh!

He was gone.

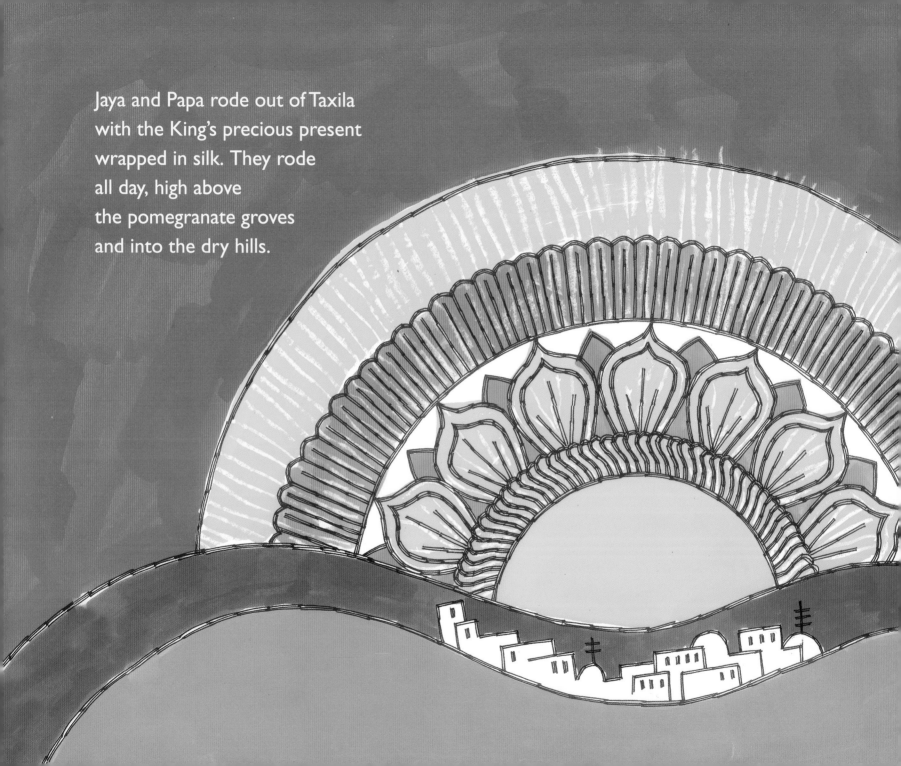

Jaya and Papa rode out of Taxila
with the King's precious present
wrapped in silk. They rode
all day, high above
the pomegranate groves
and into the dry hills.

The sun started to set, the air cooled,
and they finally stopped in a grove for the night.

But Jaya could not sleep.
She thought every shadow
was a ghost and every
sound a monster.

"I wish I weren't so scared,"
murmured Jaya.

Suddenly another coin
on Jaya's necklace
started to sparkle in the darkness.

Varoosh!

From out
of the coin leapt the goddess
Inanna, holding a crescent moon.
Its light made the shadows disappear.

"You don't have to be afraid of what's not there!" said the goddess.

"You *are* brave.
Fear only hides your bravery, little Jaya.
Sleep soundly as you dream brave thoughts."

Now the night noises and even her
Papa's snoring comforted Jaya.

"Thank you, Inanna,"
she whispered, drifting off to sleep.

"You are very welcome,"
whispered Inanna.

Then **Varoosh!**

She was gone.

The next morning, Jaya and Papa rode down sandy hills
to the wide Lion River, where they met two curious men.

"You must be bringing a birthday present to the King," said the first,
narrowing his eyes.

"A big *expensive* present!" grinned the second.

"Robbers!" whispered Papa.

"I wish these men would leave us alone," murmured Jaya.

Suddenly the third coin on Jaya's
necklace started to sparkle.

Varoosh!

From out of the coin leapt
the strongest of the gods,
Hercules, carrying a ferocious-
looking lion skin.

"Will you help us?" Jaya begged.

Hercules laughed out loud.
Placing the lion skin
in Jaya's hands, he looked
her in the eye, saying,
"You are strong enough,
little Jaya!" Then

Varoosh!

He was gone.

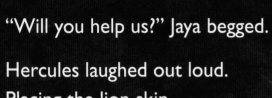

So Jaya tossed Hercules's lion skin over her shoulders and roared a great roar.

The two men trembled. Before they could move,
Jaya chased them right into the water.

Then Jaya and Papa borrowed the men's boat and sailed across the Lion River.

On the other shore they joined crowds of people on their way
to King Kanishka's palace for the royal birthday party.

When they reached the palace, King Kanishka was pacing back and forth, growling, "Where's my statue?"

"Here, King of Kings!" called Papa, as he and Jaya gently unloaded the package.

Jaya whisked off the silk wrappings.

King Kanishka looked startled for a moment.
The crowds became silent.

And then the King smiled.

"I am extremely pleased with your work.
It is something brand new.

The peaceful one
has inspired you,
and now he
inspires me.
Your wish is
my command!"

"My Mama made your birthday cake, and I want to see her right now!" said Jaya, stamping her foot.

The lords and ladies gasped. No one gave orders to King Kanishka!

"But I have so many cooks," laughed King Kanishka. "Find your mama and she's yours."

All the cooks were brought out. The line seemed to stretch forever.

Jaya looked

and looked

and looked...

...and then, she saw a red tulip!

"Mama!"

Mama ran to Papa and
Jaya and hugged them
tightly.

The big birthday party began, and there was apricot cake for everyone.

King Kanishka liked it so much that Mama gave him her secret recipe.

The next morning, as the sun rose over the Lion River, the King said to Jaya, "You have given me such wonderful gifts. So I've had a gift made just for you."

And he fastened another gold coin onto Jaya's necklace.

Jaya thanked the King. Then she, Mama, and Papa said their goodbyes and started their journey home.

Jaya looked down at the new coin sparkling on her necklace. And there, the beautiful face of the peaceful one was smiling up at her.

Learn More about Jaya's World

The Kushan Empire, 50–350 CE

The Kushan Empire was one of four great powers bringing stability to the first and second centuries alongside Rome, Persia, and the Han Empire of China. It encompassed much of present-day Afghanistan, Pakistan, Uzbekistan, and India. The Kushans descended to India from Central Asia, which had preserved much of the Greek culture brought by Alexander the Great. The Kushan Empire was a central part of the Silk Road, where people, products, and ideas—literature, technology, and medicine—traveled by caravan between China and Rome. By encouraging long-distance trade and religious tolerance, the Kushans brought peace to a vast area for three centuries.

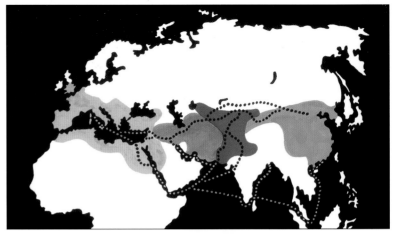

Roman Empire	Persian Empire	Kushan Empire	Han Empire	Silk Road

Kushan Coins

Ancient rulers proclaimed their power on coins. On Kushan coins we can read the name of the king, see his special costume, crown, and symbol (or *tamgha*), and learn which gods and goddesses he considered important. Thirty-three Greco-Roman, Iranian, and Indian gods and goddesses appear in the Kushan coin pantheon.

King Kanishka, wearing boots and making an offering at an altar. Gold.

Buddha, in one of the first pictures of him in human form. Bronze.

Shiva, Indian god of creation and destruction. Bronze.

Inanna, Iranian goddess of wisdom and fertility. Bronze.

Hercules, Greco-Roman god of strength. Bronze.

Here is King Kanishka's *tamgha* symbol. People would recognize it like a logo, even those who could not read. Can you find it on the coins?

The Silk Road

The Silk Road was a network of land and sea trade routes extending four thousand miles across Eurasia. Two-humped Bactrian camels were popular because they could walk across deserts without needing much water. Traders and their goods flowed through the Kushan Empire, bringing wealth and new ideas with them. The Silk Road was an ancient worldwide web.

Products flowing East to West:

Silk: The Greeks called silk "woven wind," and the Romans loved to wear it.

Spices: Pepper, cinnamon, cloves, ginger, nutmeg, and saffron were traded.

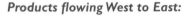

Products flowing West to East:

Gold: Many Roman coins have been found in India, often used in jewelry.

Horses: Fast and powerful, Central Asian horses were dubbed "heavenly horses" by the Chinese.

Buddhism

Buddhism began in India in the fifth century BCE. During the Kushan Empire, Buddhism was changing. The altruistic ideal of the bodhisattva became more important. The first statues of bodhisattvas were modeled on Kushan aristocrats. Buddhism spread along the Silk Road to China, and Buddhism's tolerance made the Kushan Empire move more smoothly. Offerings to monasteries funded thousands of *stupa* monuments, which were covered with carvings telling the Buddha's life story. King Kanishka is credited with calling a council where many Buddhist scriptures were collected and arranged.

This fragment of *The Song of Lake Anavatapta*, a Buddhist scripture extolling generosity, was found in Afghanistan and dates to the first century. It is written on birch bark in *kharoshti* script and reads from right to left.

Kanishka and His Great Stupa

King Kanishka built a truly amazing *stupa* at his capital in Peshawar. Over six hundred feet high, it was the tallest structure people had ever seen, a wonder of the ancient world. From its top fluttered long silk streamers. Travelers visited it for over five hundred years, and such stupas inspired the pagodas of China and Japan.

Kushan Style

Well-dressed Kushan women wore wreaths of leaves and flowers on their heads. Long earrings and ankle bracelets were also fashionable.

This bilingual inscription from a Kushan coin uses Greek letters and the Indian *kharoshti* script to write "King of Kings."

ΒΑCΙΛΕΥC ΒΑCΙΛΕWΝ

Learn More

▶ Episode 3 of the BBC's *Story of India* includes much information on the Kushan world and an animation of the great stupa: www.youtube.com/watch?v=mDofYtYO5fL

▶ *A Rough Guide to Kushan History* has many resources: www.kushan.org

▶ *Coinindia* has a gallery of Kushan coins: coinindia.com/galleries-kushan.html

Mama's Apricot Cake

Bring all ingredients to room temperature.
Preheat oven to 350°F.

Beat until fluffy in a large bowl:
1¼ cups sugar
1 stick (½ cup) butter

Beat in:
4 eggs, one at a time
1 teaspoon vanilla extract
½ teaspoon almond extract

Mix separately:
2 cups sifted flour
1 cup almond meal
1 teaspoon baking powder
½ teaspoon salt

Alternating with flour mixture, stir into butter mixture just until moistened:
4 tablespoons milk (for canned fruit)
or ½ cup milk (for fresh)
or ¾ cup milk (for dried)

Dice and fold in:
5 fresh apricots, dredged in flour
or
1½ cups of canned or dried apricots

Pour into greased 9-inch cake pan and bake at 350°F for around 50 minutes. Make sure the top starts to brown and the center is cooked. Let cool and turn onto plate.

Topping
Pit and halve six large sweet apricots, sauté with 1 tablespoon butter until they start to soften but keep their shape, and arrange on top of cake.
In remaining liquid, stir in 2 tablespoons or so of sugar and heat until it caramelizes into a glaze, adding fruit juice or puree as necessary to thin. Drizzle the glaze over the apricot halves. Serve and enjoy.